S0-AAN-321

Things that are most in the world

in the world

Library Media Center
Jefferson School
Huntington, New York

WRITTEN BY Judi Barrett

Things
that
are
most
in the world

illustrated BY John Nickle

SCHOLASTIC INC.
New York Toronto London Auckland Sydney
Mexico City New Delhi Hong Kong

No part of this publication may be reproduced
in whole or in part, or stored in a retrieval system,
or transmitted in any form or by any means, electronic,
mechanical, photocopying, recording, or otherwise,
without written permission of the publisher.
For information regarding permission,
write to Atheneum Books for Young Readers,
Simon and Schuster Children's Publishing Division,
1230 Avenue of the Americas, New York, NY 10020.

ISBN 0-439-13353-X

Text copyright © 1998 by Judi Barrett.
Illustrations copyright © 1998 by John Nickle.
All rights reserved.
Published by Scholastic Inc., 555 Broadway, New York, NY 10012,
by arrangement with Atheneum Books for Young Readers,
Simon and Schuster Children's Publishing Division. SCHOLASTIC
and associated logos are trademarks and/or registered
trademarks of Scholastic Inc.

12 11 10 9 8 7 6 5 4 3 2 1   9/9 0 1 2 3 4/0

Printed in the U.S.A.   08

First Scholastic printing, January 2000

Book design by Ann Bobco
The text of this book is set in Gill Sans Bold and Psycho Progressive.
The illustrations are rendered in acrylic paint.

To things that are the most, the least,
and everything in between
— J. B.

To Jana
"Who's the monkey?"
— J. N.

The

wiggliest

thing in the world

is

a snake ice-skating.

The
silliest
thing in the world

is

a chicken

in a frog costume.

The

quietest

thing in the world

is

a worm

chewing peanut butter.

The prickliest

thing in the world

is

the inside of a pincushion.

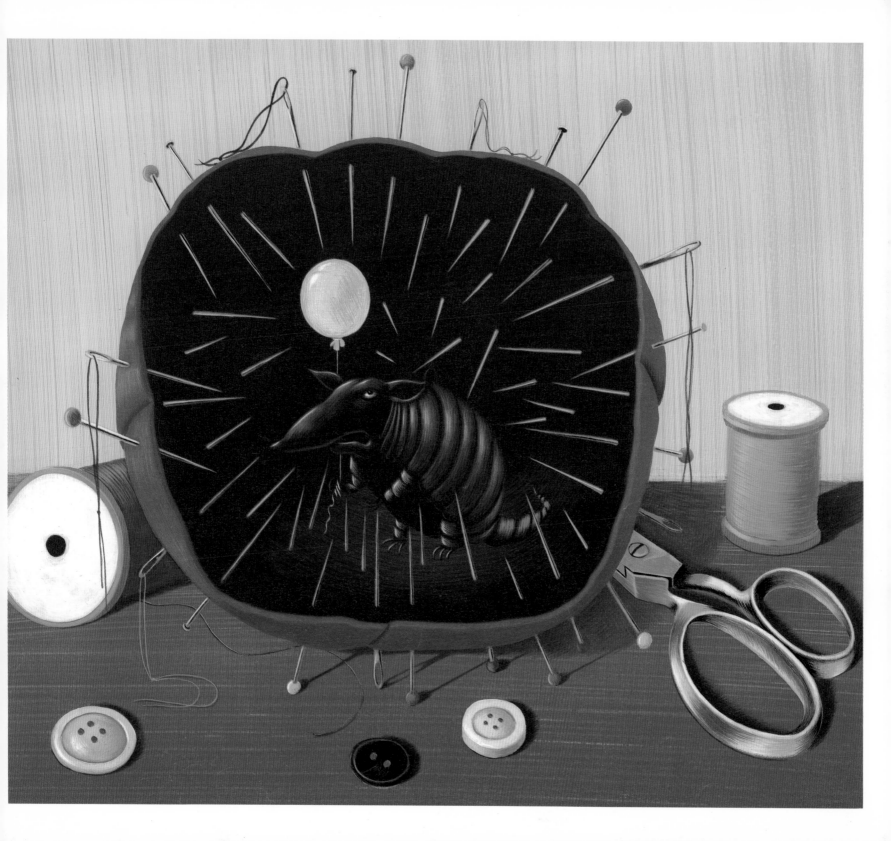

The

hottest

thing in the world

is

a fire-breathing dragon

eating a pepperoni pizza.

The

oddest

thing in the world

is

an ant windsurfing

in a bowl of pea soup.

The

teensie-weensiest

thing in the world

is

a newborn flea.

The

longest

thing in the world

is

what you'd have

if you tied every single strand

of spaghetti together

end to end.

The

jumpiest

thing in the world

is

two thousand two hundred twenty-two toads

on a trampoline.

The
smelliest
thing in the world

is

a skunk convention.

The

stickiest

thing in the world

is

a 400,000-pound wad

of bubble gum.

The
heaviest
thing in the world

is

a Tyrannosaurus rex

weighing himself.

And the

highest

thing in the world

is

the very top of the sky.

The

_____**est**

thing in the world

is

_____●

Library Media Center
Jefferson School
Huntington, New York

Photocopy this page and write and draw your own thing that's most in the world.